JIMMIE JOHNSON

Heidi
Krumenauer

Mitchell Lane

P.O. Box 196
Hockessin, Delaware 19707
Visit us on the web: www.mitchelllane.com
Comments? email us: mitchelllane@mitchelllane.com

Mitchell Lane

Printing 1 2 3 4 5 6 7 8 9

A Robbie Reader
Contemporary Biography

Abigail Breslin
Aly and AJ
Brenda Song
Dakota Fanning
Demi Lovato
Dr. Seuss
Eli Manning
Jaden Smith
Jimmie Johnson
Jordin Sparks
Miley Cyrus
Selena Gomez
Syd Hoff
Tony Hawk
Albert Pujols
Amanda Bynes
Brittany Murphy
Dale Earnhardt Jr.
Donovan McNabb
Dwayne "The Rock" Johnson
Emily Osment
Jamie Lynn Spears
Johnny Gruelle
LeBron James
Miranda Cosgrove
Shaquille O'Neal
Tiki Barber
Alex Rodriguez
Ashley Tisdale
Charles Schulz
David Archuleta
Drake Bell & Josh Peck
Dylan & Cole Sprouse
Hilary Duff
Jesse McCartney
Jonas Brothers
Mia Hamm
Raven-Symone
Story of Harley-Davidson
Tom Brady

Library of Congress Cataloging-in-Publication Data
Krumenauer, Heidi.
Jimmie Johnson / by Heidi Krumenauer.
p. cm. — (A Robbie reader)
Includes bibliographical references and index.
ISBN 978-1-58415-756-4 (library bound)
1. Johnson, Jimmie, 1975- —Juvenile literature. 2. Automobile racing drivers—United States—Biography—Juvenile literature. I. Title.
GV1032.J54K78 2009
796.72092—dc22
[B]

2009004525

ABOUT THE AUTHOR: Heidi Krumenauer has written more than 1,100 newspaper and magazine articles. She is a regular contributor to several print and online publications, and she has contributed chapters to nonfiction book projects. Heidi's first book, *Why Does Grandma Have a Wibble?,* was released in 2007. She also wrote *Brett Favre, Rihanna, Joe Flacco,* and *Sean Kingston* for Mitchell Lane Publishers. Heidi graduated from the University of Wisconsin-Platteville with a degree in Technical Communications Management. She works in upper management for a Fortune 400 insurance company. Heidi and her husband, Jeff, are raising their two sons, Noah and Payton, in Southern Wisconsin.

PUBLISHER'S NOTE: The following story has been thoroughly researched and to the best of our knowledge represents a true story. While every possible effort has been made to ensure accuracy, the publisher will not assume liability for damages caused by inaccuracies in the data, and makes no warranty on the accuracy of the information contained herein. This story has not been authorized or endorsed by Jimmie Johnson.

DISCLAIMER: The sport of auto racing or motorcycle racing should not be attempted without extensive training, experience, proper protective gear, and professional assistance. These are high risk and dangerous sports and may result in or cause serious injury to oneself or another and may even cause death. Always consult with a trained racing professional before trying these sports. Mitchell Lane Publishers shall not be held liable for any injuries to or damages caused by individuals attempting this sport or any other daredevil feats displayed by Jimmie Johnson. *Always Put Safety First.*

PLB

TABLE OF CONTENTS

Words in **bold** type can be found in the glossary.

Jimmie Johnson celebrates his third NASCAR Sprint Cup Series Championship on November 16, 2008. The #48 Lowe's Hendrick Motorsports team joined Jimmie for the celebration at the last race of the season at Homestead-Miami Speedway.

CHAPTER ONE

Three-peat Champion

It was more than 110 degrees inside his car, but Jimmie Johnson wasn't worried about the heat. He was thinking about the big prize—the 2008 **NASCAR** Sprint Cup **Championship** (CHAM-pee-un-ship). For the next three and a half hours, he would try to keep his racecar on the oval track without wrecking. He would also try to keep his **points** lead over Carl Edwards. During this last race of the season at Homestead-Miami Speedway, there was a chance that Carl could win the **NASCAR Sprint Cup Series**.

In 2006, Jimmie won his first NASCAR Cup Championship. He did it again in 2007. In the 2008 season, Jimmie was again a leader on the track. With the points earned from seven wins, 15 Top 5s, and 22 Top 10s, Jimmie was in line to win his third championship.

Jimmie started the race in 30th position, driving the #48 Lowe's Chevrolet Impala SS. He

With one week to go in the 2008 NASCAR Sprint Cup season, Jimmie Johnson leads the pack at the Checker O'Reilly Auto Parts 500 race at Phoenix International Speedway. Jimmie started on the **pole**, led 217 laps, and ended the race in Victory Lane.

was one of four drivers of the Hendrick Racing Team. Carl Edwards, driver of the #99 Office Depot Ford Fusion, was hot on his trail.

Although Carl won the race and Jimmie finished 15th, Jimmie was able to keep the points lead over Carl—by just 69 for the season. Only one other person in the history of NASCAR had won the championship three years in a row. Cale Yarborough (YAR-bur-oh) won the NASCAR Cup in 1976, 1977, and 1978.

At the end of 2008, Jimmie could count 40 trophies from his victories in NASCAR's Cup Series. Where does he keep them? Jimmie says that only a couple of them are at his home. The rest are on display at his race shop in Charlotte, where fans can see them when they take a tour. "We keep them where people can enjoy them," Jimmie told *Sports Illustrated Kids* in 2008.

Even with all the fame and trophies, Jimmie considers himself an average guy. He told *The Sporting News*, "I grew up in a very simple home, a very simple background, and to be able to do what I'm able to do today, I'm very honored."

Driver Kyle Petty says Jimmie is one of the greatest drivers in racing history. He compares

Jimmie is proud of being a three-time NASCAR champion, but he knows that being the best comes with a lot of hard work by himself and his crew.

Cale Yarborough, right, celebrated with Jimmie at the NASCAR Sprint Cup Series Awards Ceremony in New York City on December 5, 2008. Jimmie and Yarborough are the only two NASCAR drivers to win championships three years in a row.

Jimmie to racing legends Jeff Gordon, Dale Earnhardt, and Kyle's father, Richard Petty. Each of those drivers has also won NASCAR championships. Winston Cup Champion Dale Jarrett told *The Roanoke Times* in 2008, "When you think about Jimmie Johnson's name, you have to think about championships."

Jimmie, right, his brother Jarit, left, and their father Gary, back, watch as Jessie Johnson, their 13-year-old brother, races his Bandolero series car at Lowe's Motor Speedway in 2002.

CHAPTER TWO

California Boy

Jimmie Kenneth Johnson was born on September 17, 1975, in the San Diego suburb of El Cajon, California. His father, Gary, worked for a tire company and coached **motocross**. His mother, Cathy, drove a school bus. Jimmie and his two younger brothers, Jarit and Jessie, grew up in a two-bedroom home with their parents. When Jimmie was young, he would go camping and racing with his family. His dad helped prepare the motocross tracks. His mother usually ran the refreshment stand.

When Jimmie was four years old, his dad put some old parts together and built Jimmie his first bike for Christmas. It wasn't just any bike—it was a motorbike! Jimmie wasn't even in kindergarten, and he was racing motorcycles in the California desert.

Jimmie's racing career started on **50cc** motorcycles when he was five years old. When he was seven, Jimmie took a dare from his friend, Rick Johnson. Jimmie's bike flew 65 feet through the air off a six-foot jump. His bike landed safely, but then skidded into a crash. Jimmie never saw a thing. He was too scared to open his eyes. "That was when I knew he had the talent to go into the corner at 190 mph [miles per hour]," says Rick, a seven-time champion in motocross and **supercross**.

That stunt didn't stop Jimmie. When he was eight years old, he was racing 60cc motorbikes. He missed the end of the season because of a broken knee. He'd won so many times during the season, he only needed to drive one lap to win the championship. Jimmie raced with a cast on his leg and won the points title.

Jimmie enjoyed watching Indy driver Rick Mears when he was growing up. He was also a fan of stock car racers Cale Yarborough, Bobby and Davey Allison, and Dale Earnhardt. Because there weren't many stock car races

In August 2007, Jimmie and his wife, Chandra, visited Granite Hills High School in El Cajon, California—the school Jimmie graduated from in 1993. They promoted the Jimmie Johnson Foundation and delivered equipment from his sponsor, Lowe's.

where Jimmie lived, he didn't get to experience that side of racing until later.

Jimmie's heart has always been in racing, but he also enjoyed playing water sports. When Jimmie attended Granite Hills High School, he played water polo, was on the swim team, and enjoyed surfing. He even raced jet skis! Jimmie loved to jump off things. "I remember being real young and jumping off a bridge overpass when we were camping out at the desert," he told *The Roanoke Times*. Jimmie has always loved a thrill!

Jimmie made his Craftsman Truck Series debut on August 20, 2008, at Bristol Speedway. The truck is owned by New England Patriots receiver Randy Moss.

Jimmie makes a pit stop in the O'Reilly 200 at Bristol with his #81 Lowe's/Kobalt Tools Chevrolet. This truck is much smaller than the off-road trucks he raced as a teen.

CHAPTER THREE

From Bikes to Trucks and Cars

In his early teens, Jimmie started taking an interest in off-road racing. When he was fifteen, he began racing in the Mickey Thompson Entertainment Group Stadium Racing Series. He was their youngest driver ever!

After graduating from Granite Hills in 1993, Jimmie spent several years racing trucks, both off-road and in stadiums. He won his first championship at seventeen. By the time he moved into the NASCAR Series in 1999, he had earned six major championships, 25 victories, more than 100 Top 3 finishes, and Rookie of the Year in three different **leagues**.

At age nineteen, Jimmie raced in the Baja 1000 in the deserts of Mexico. This off-road race—the world's longest nonstop desert race—includes motorcycles, trucks, and other race vehicles. Jimmie had been racing for more than 20 hours when he fell asleep behind the wheel. His 4,000-pound truck rolled 300 feet down a cliff. It landed on its side in the bottom of a sand wash.

Jimmie was stranded for almost two days. He lived on tuna fish, granola bars, and water—supplies that he kept in his truck. That was a turning point in his life. He realized that he needed to learn how to push the vehicle he

Before the 2007 NASCAR season, Jimmie was one of four drivers who would take turns behind the wheel of the #91 Lowe's Riley-Matthews Motorsports Pontiac Riley at the Rolex 24 Daytona. The 24-hour race is held on a 3.56-mile combined road course and **tri-oval** track.

In 2002, Jimmie teamed up with Jeff Gordon and biker Colin Edwards for the ROC (Race of Champions) Nations Cup. The team won the international race, which was held in the Canary Islands.

was driving but bring it home safely. Jimmie started thinking seriously about a career in racing.

When Jimmie was twenty-one, he moved to Charlotte, North Carolina. He spent a lot of time trying to meet people who could help him in his career. In 1998, he started driving for the American Speed Association (ASA). It was the first time he had raced on pavement. During his first race, he spun his car twelve times. After a while, he settled down and got used to the car. Jimmie finished fourth in the ASA championship points race, and he was named Rookie of the Year.

Chad Knaus, right, and Jimmie Johnson talk shop before a race. It's important to have a good relationship with your crew chief because he plays a big role in helping the driver win. A crew chief is compared to a head coach of other professional sports. Chad Knaus has been Jimmie Johnson's crew chief since 2002.

CHAPTER FOUR

NASCAR's Young Gun

In 1999, Jimmie started racing in the **NASCAR Busch Series**. He raced three times during his first year. The next year, he raced five times. From 1999 to 2001, he won only one race.

In 2001, Jimmie raced three times in the NASCAR Cup Series. The next year, he began racing full-time. Guess who owned Jimmie's car. . . . Jeff Gordon! Jimmie started that season on the pole of the Daytona 500 and finished in 15th position. He finished the season fifth in points.

In 2003 and 2004, Jimmie came close to winning the championships. He was second in points. In 2005, he ended the season fifth in points. Then his luck changed!

After hitting the wall at the Allstate 400 in Indianapolis Motor Speedway in 2007, Jimmie leaped from his car to avoid the flames. Racing is a dangerous sport, but many times the drivers escape injuries—even in accidents like this one.

Jimmie started the 2006 season by winning the Daytona 500. He was also named NASCAR Driver of the Year in 2006. And that's not all! He won his first **NASCAR Nextel Cup** Championship. He set a record by winning $15,952,125 during the season. Jimmie could keep only a portion of it. The rest went to his team and team owner, Rick Hendrick.

Jimmie has learned a lot about racing from four-time NASCAR Cup Champion Jeff Gordon.

On the track, Jeff Gordon (left) is a teammate, but he is also a competitor—trying to beat Jimmie to the finish line. Off the track, Jimmie and Jeff are good friends.

"Honestly, I learn something from him all the time," Jimmie told *The Sporting News* in 2004. "We don't sit down and have meetings where I'm the student. He really teaches by example."

Jimmie doesn't take his three-time NASCAR championships for granted. He knows it's important to stay on top of his game. Jimmie thinks he can be even better, and he thinks his team can always be better, too.

Jimmie trades in his racing uniform for a suit to take his wife, Chandra, to the NASCAR Sprint Cup Series Awards Ceremony in New York City.

CHAPTER FIVE

Jimmie—Off the Track

During racing season, Jimmie doesn't get much time to relax. He is usually preparing for the next race, going to meetings, or doing interviews. When he has free time, he likes to be on the water. Jimmie shared details of his personal life on the Lowe's Racing web site. "I live on a lake in North Carolina, and when I'm not working, you'll find me out on my boat or one of my jet skis catching up with my friends and family," he says. He also likes to go mountain biking, snowboarding, skiing, fishing, golfing, and relaxing on his couch, watching his favorite television shows. "It's nice to just kick back and relax every once in a while," he admits.

Racecar drivers are athletes, and they must spend a lot of time preparing their bodies

When he's not on the track, Jimmie is busy meeting his fans and signing autographs. He high-fives five-year-old fan Tyler Walkup during an autograph session at Indianapolis Motor Speedway.

for 36 weeks of racing. Jimmie belongs to a gym and exercises five or six days a week. During racing season, though, he doesn't have much time to work out. He tries to find time to go mountain biking. "It's a great workout, and I enjoy being outside. In addition, it might sound funny to someone that has never raced before, but you get a pretty good workout racing cars," Jimmie says. Still, he has a hard time turning down his favorite food—a cheeseburger from In-N-Out Burger—and sneaking ice cream late at night.

Jimmie's life might look glamorous, but he wants people to know that he's just a normal guy who has a really cool job. "I still do laundry, pay bills, wash dishes, do yard work, all the same things that everyone else has to do. Many people think that as drivers, we have people that do all of those things, but many of us don't. We're just the average next door neighbors," Jimmie says.

Jimmie married model Chandra Janway on December 11, 2004. They live in Charlotte, North Carolina. They have two small dogs, but someday Jimmie would like a big dog like a lab or greyhound.

In February 2006, Jimmie launched his weekly radio show on XM Satellite, *Jimmie Johnson . . . "Not What You Expected."* That same month, he started the Jimmie Johnson Foundation. It helps to build homes for families living in poor conditions. It also supports other

Jimmie gets ready to qualify his racecar, the #48 Lowe's Jimmie Johnson Foundation Chevrolet, for the Pepsi 500 at the Auto Club Speedway in Fontana, California, in 2008. Jimmie's uniform matched his car, which sported the logo for the Foundation he launched in 2006.

groups such as Make-A-Wish, American Red Cross, Victory Junction Gang Camp, and Habitat for Humanity.

In 2007 and 2008, Jimmie drove a car with a special Jimmie Johnson Foundation paint scheme. It must have been good luck, because he won both years!

CHRONOLOGY

1975 Jimmie Kenneth Johnson is born on September 17.

1992 Jimmie wins his first stadium motocross championship in the Mickey Thompson Entertainment Group Stadium Racing Series.

1993 Jimmie graduates from Granite Hills High School.

1998 He is named the ASA Pat Schauer Memorial Rookie of the Year.

1999 He starts racing in the NASCAR Busch Series.

2001 He starts three races in the NASCAR Cup Series.

2002 In his official rookie season, he races full-time in the NASCAR Cup Series.

2003 Jimmie wins the Nextel All-Star Challenge. He finishes second in points for the NASCAR Cup Series.

2004 Jimmie finishes second in points for the NASCAR Cup Series. He marries model Chandra Janway on December 11.

2005 Jimmie finishes fifth in points for the NASCAR Cup Series.

2006 On February 19, Jimmie wins the Daytona 500. He wins his first NASCAR Nextel Cup Championship. The Jimmie Johnson Foundation is launched. He also starts his radio show, *Jimmie Johnson . . . "Not What You Expected."*

2007 He wins his second NASCAR Nextel Cup Championship.

2008 Jimmie wins his third NASCAR Cup Championship. He is only the second person in history to do that. Jimmie makes his debut in the Craftsman Truck Series in August.

2009 Going into the tenth race of the season, Jimmie has won one race, has four top five finishes, six top ten finishes, and ranks third in the points.

CAREER STATS

Year	Races	Wins	Poles	Top 5	Top 10	DNF*	Finished
2001	3	0	0	0	0	1	52nd
2002	36	3	5	6	21	3	5th
2003	36	3	2	14	20	3	2nd
2004	36	8	3	20	23	7	2nd
2005	36	4	2	13	22	5	5th
2006	36	5	1	13	24	1	1st
2007	36	10	4	20	24	4	1st
2008	36	7	6	15	22	1	1st
Totals	**255**	**40**	**23**	**101**	**156**	**25**	

*DNF = Did not finish the race

FIND OUT MORE

Books

Gitlin, Marty. *Jimmy Johnson: Racing Champ.* Berkeley Heights, NJ: Enslow Publishers, 2008.

Lemasters, Ron, Jr. *Jimmie Johnson: A Desert Rat's Race to Stardom.* Minneapolis, MN: Motorbooks, 2004.

Sports Illustrated Kids: "The SIK Q&A." February 2008, p. 28.

Works Consulted

James, Brant. "All About Jimmie." *St. Petersburg Times,* November 21, 2006. http://www.sptimes.com/2006/11/21/Sports/All_about_Jimmie.shtml

Jimmie Johnson . . . "Not What You Expected" http://www.xmradio.com/jimmiejohnson/

Lemasters, Ron. "Johnson, Gordon, HMS Take Home Largest of Hauls." NASCAR.com, December 4, 2007. http://www.nascar.com/2007/news/business/12/04/jjohnson.jgordon.winnings/index.html

Long, Dustin. "Interview with Jimmie." *The Roanoke Times,* March 30, 2008. http://www.roanoke.com/sports/racing/wb/156406

Long, Dustin. "Lord of Rings: Jimmie Johnson Finalizes Sprint Cup Trilogy by Finishing 15th." *The Roanoke Times,* November 17, 2008. http://www.roanoke.com/sports/racing/wb/184531

FIND OUT MORE

Lowe's Racing Website: Jimmie's FAQ
http://www.lowesracing.com/jimmie/faq

McCarter, Mark. "That Glint in His Eye: Jimmie Johnson, A Prime Example of the New Generation of Drivers, Is Focused on Getting to the Top of the NASCAR Heap." *The Sporting News,* February 16, 2004. http://findarticles.com/p/articles/mi_m1208/is_/ai_113299087

NASCAR Teleconference Transcript: Jimmie Johnson, October 14, 2008. http://www.restrictorplatethis.com/section/jimmie-johnson

Rodman, Dave. "Top Ten Questions with . . . Jimmie Johnson." NASCAR.com, November 22, 2005. http://www.nascar.com/2005/news/headlines/cup/11/22/jjohnson.10.questions/index.html

Ryan, Nate. "Johnson Zips Past Misconceptions, Zeroes In on Title." USAToday.com, May 28, 2006. http://www.usatoday.com/sports/motor/nascar/2006-05-25-johnson-cover_x.htm

Woody, Larry. "The Child Is the Father to the Man: Rookie Jimmie Johnson Is Repaying His Co-owner Jeff Gordon's Faith in Him by Challenging the Four-time Champion for the Winston Cup Title." *Auto Racing Digest,* October–November 2002. http://findarticles.com/p/articles/mi_m0FCH/is_/ai_90217149

On the Internet

Jimmie Johnson Foundation
http://www.jimmiejohnsonfoundation.org

Lowe's Racing
www.lowesracing.com

NASCAR
www.nascar.com

Official Site of Hendrick Motorsports NASCAR Racing Team
www.hendrickmotorsports.com

Photo Credits: Cover, pp. 1, 3, 9–Rusty Jarrett/Getty Images for NASCAR; p. 4–Sam Greenwood/Getty Images for NASCAR; p. 6–AP Photo/Paul Connors; p. 8–AP Photo/Matt Slocum; p. 10–AP Photo/Chuck Burton; p. 13–Kent Horner/Getty Images; p. 14 (top)–Bristol Motor Speedway/cc-nc-sa-2.0; p. 14 (bottom)–John Harrelson/Getty Images; p. 16–Chris Putnam/WireImage; p. 18–Jason Smith/Getty Images for NASCAR; p. 20–AP Photo/Scott Anderson; p. 21–AP Photo/Mark Humphrey; p. 22–Brad Barket/Getty Images for NASCAR; p. 24–AP Photo/Tom Strattman; p. 26–Robert Laberge/Getty Images.

GLOSSARY

50cc (FIF-tee see see)—A 50 cubic centimeter engine; 60cc is a larger and faster engine.

championship (CHAM-pee-un-ship)—A series of competitions to determine an overall winner.

league (LEEG)—A group of teams that compete against one another.

motocross (MOH-toh-kross)—Outdoor off-road motorcycle racing with jumps, corners, and obstacles.

NASCAR—National Association for Stock Car Auto Racing.

NASCAR Busch Series—NASCAR's "minor league," it was renamed the Nationwide Series in 2008. Drivers usually start in this league before moving up to the Sprint Cup.

NASCAR Nextel Cup—The NASCAR Cup Series, whose sponsor became Nextel in 2008. Sprint Nextel Corporation was the sponsor from 2004 to 2007. It was known as the Winston Cup Series from 1971 to 2003.

NASCAR Sprint Cup Series—Also known as the Sprint Cup or Cup Series, this is the top racing series for NASCAR, with a 36-race season starting in February.

point—A scoring unit. Drivers are awarded points for leading a lap, leading the most laps in a race, position at the end of the race, and winning the race. The driver with the most points at the end of a season wins the championship.

pole—The lead starting position of a race.

rookie—Someone in his or her first year in a league.

supercross—A type of off-road motorcycle race held in a large indoor stadium.

tri-oval—A nearly oval racetrack with one long straightaway and three banked curves.

INDEX